Angus Rides the Goods Train

Dedicated to the memory of Irma Hadzimuratovic (1988–1995),
whose courage continues to inspire.
A. D.

For Ian Jack
C. R.

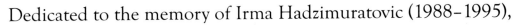

ANGUS RIDES THE GOODS TRAIN
A PICTURE CORGI BOOK 978 0 552 56919 4
First published in Great Britain by the Penguin Group, 1996

Picture Corgi edition published 2004
This Picture Corgi edition published 2013

1 3 5 7 9 10 8 6 4 2

Picture Corgi Books are published by Random House Children's Publishers UK,
61–63 Uxbridge Road, London W5 5SA

www.randomhousechildrens.co.uk
www.randomhouse.co.uk

Addresses for companies within The Random House Group Limited can be found at:
www.randomhouse.co.uk/offices.htm

THE RANDOM HOUSE GROUP Limited Reg. No. 954009

A CIP catalogue record for this book is available from the British Library.

Printed in China

The Random House Group Limited supports the Forest Stewardship Council® (FSC®), the leading
international forest-certification organisation. Our books carrying the FSC label are printed on
FSC®-certified paper. FSC is the only forest-certification scheme supported by the leading
environmental organisations, including Greenpeace. Our paper procurement policy
can be found at www.randomhouse.co.uk/environment

FSC
MIX
Paper from
responsible sources
FSC® C104723

Angus Rides the
Goods Train

Alan Durant

Illustrated by Chris Riddell

Picture Corgi

That night Angus rode the goods train.

He awoke to the sound of clunking and chinking.

And there it was.

"All aboard!" called the driver – and Angus climbed up on to the train.

He saw milk and honey and rice and a huge tank of water to make steam for the train.

"Where are we going?" he asked.

"Somewhere very important," said the driver. "Far away. Far, far away."

And with a whistle and a whoosh they were off.

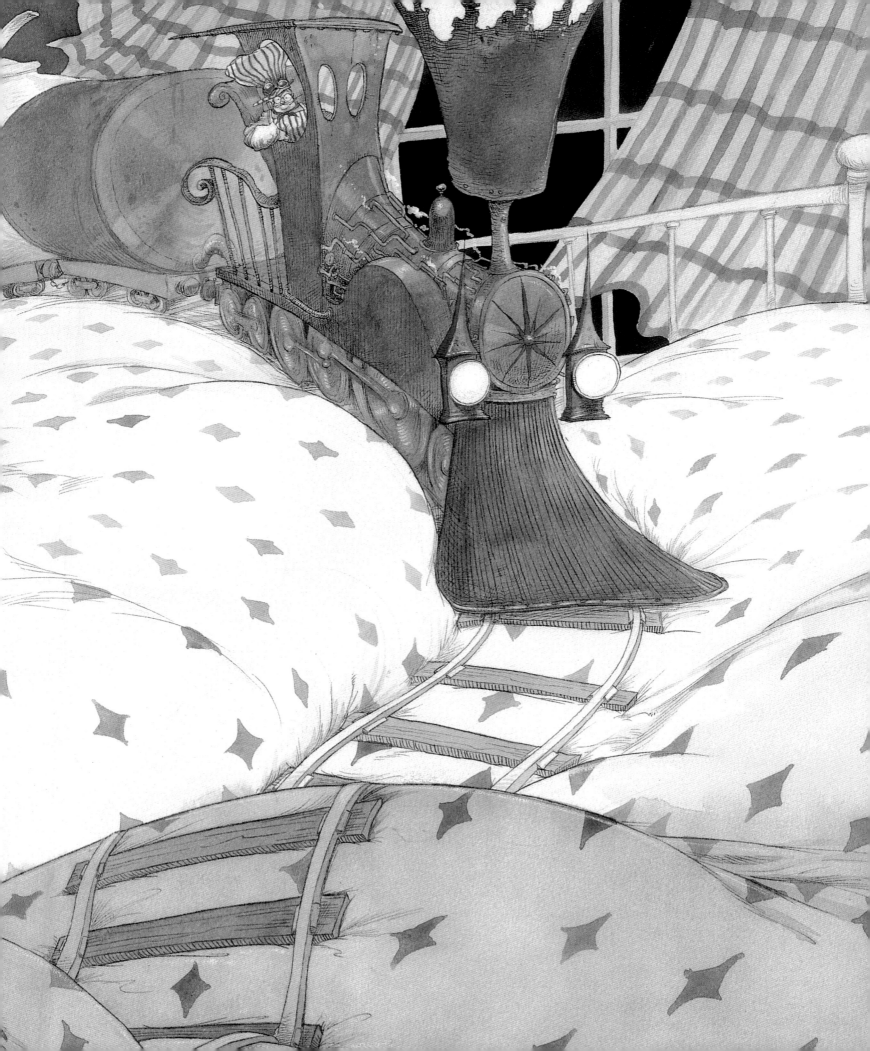

Away they sped across the land and over the sea, in and out of towns and cities, up and down hills and mountains, through fields and valleys and forests thick and lush with trees . . .

The wind swept through Angus's hair and his heart was happy to be going far, far away to somewhere so important.

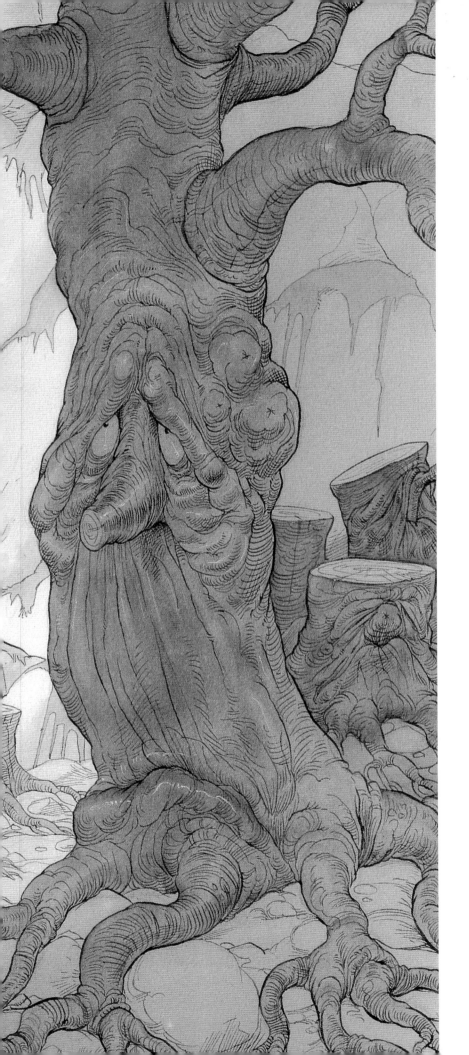

Then the landscape changed.

They came to a thin forest of
stunted and withered trees.

"Help us. Help us, please,"
groaned the trees. "We need water."

Angus's heart went out to the trees.
"Oh, let's stop and help them,"
he said. "We have lots of water."

But the driver would not stop.
"We have no water to spare," he
said. "We have far to go."

And on they sped once more . . .

. . . Until they came to a place where there were lots of cages.

In each of them was a bear. The bears shook their heads and they pawed at the bars.

"We are going mad," they wailed. "We are starving."

Angus's heart went out to the bears. "Stop!" he cried. "We must stop and help. We have honey."

But the driver would not stop. "We have no honey to spare," he said.

And on they raced into the darkness . . .

. . . Away from the towns and the woods and the fields, away from the rivers and the trees and the grass, headlong into the desert they rushed.

And there by a dune sat a mother and her crying baby.

"Help us, please," moaned the mother. "I have no milk for my baby."

Angus's heart went out to the mother and her baby. "Yes," he said, "I will help. I can give you milk."

But the driver would not stop.

Now they came to a terrible place,
where the houses were all broken
and the fields were full of holes.
By the track stood a girl.

"Oh, please, can you help me?" she
called. "I have lost my mother and
my father. And I am so hungry."

Angus's heart went out to the girl.
"Stop!" he cried. "Driver, please
stop. We have rice to give."

But the driver drove on.

At last, as dawn broke, they arrived in a beautiful green valley.
The driver slowed down and said, "There, these are the people who our goods are for:
the king and his courtiers. Every day, I bring milk and honey and rice for their breakfast."

"But there are so few of them for so much food," said Angus.
"They are very important," said the driver.
Then he put on the brake and stopped the train beside the table. He bowed very low.
"Breakfast, Your Majesty!" he said, but . . .

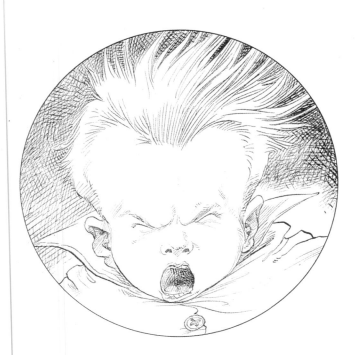

. . . "No!" cried Angus. "No, no, this is not right!" And he pushed the driver down from the train.

Angus pulled on the lever and the wheels started to turn, and he drove the goods train away from the table, away from the king and the courtiers waiting to eat, away from the driver, out of the dawn and back into the dark . . .

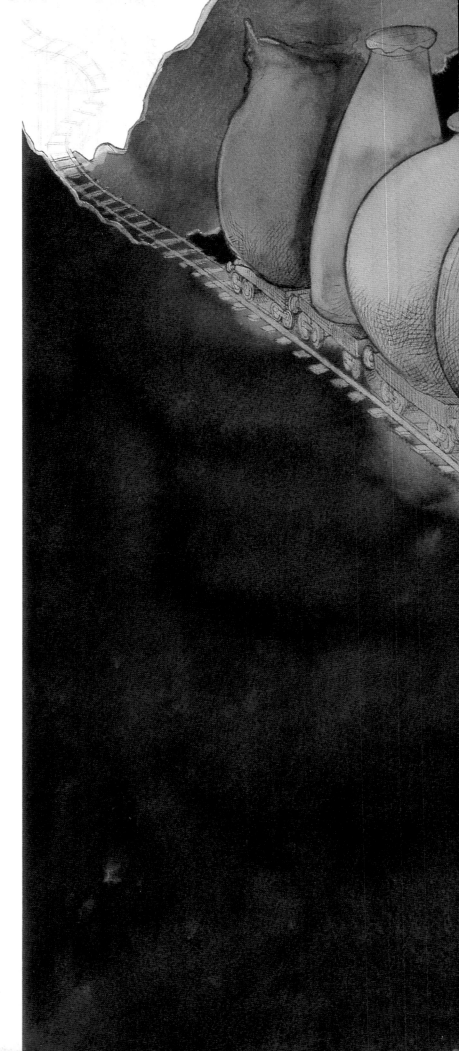

He came to the terrible place, where the girl still stood.
"Climb aboard," said Angus, "and have some rice."

On into the desert they rode, and Angus gave milk
to the mother and her baby.

Angus gave honey to the caged bears.

Angus poured water
on the roots of the
withering trees.

When Angus arrived home to
his bed, the goods train was
empty and Angus was full of joy.

At breakfast, on the television, Angus saw a picture of his friend, and he watched as a man explained why they could not help, could not give, could not save.

"One day," vowed Angus, "I will drive the goods train."

Always and Forever

Debi Gliori
Alan Durant

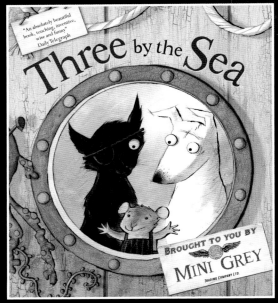

"An absolutely beautiful book, touching, inventive, wise and funny"
Daily Telegraph

Three by the Sea

BROUGHT TO YOU BY
MINI GREY
TRADING COMPANY LTD

By the author of *War Horse*

michael morpurgo

THE
RAINBOW
BEAR

Illustrated by
Michael Foreman

By the author of *War Horse*

michael morpurgo

LITTLE
ALBATROSS

Illustrated by Michael Foreman